Bamboo & Friends
The Tree

by Felicia Law
illustrated by Claire Philpott

Editor: Jacqueline A. Wolfe
Page Production: Tracy Davies
Creative Director: Keith Griffin
Editorial Director: Carol Jones
Managing Editor: Catherine Neitge

First American edition published in 2006 by
Picture Window Books
5115 Excelsior Boulevard
Suite 232
Minneapolis, MN 55416
877-845-8392
www.picturewindowbooks.com

Printed in the United States of America.

Library of Congress Cataloging-in-Publication Data
Law, Felicia.
The tree / by Felicia Law ; illustrated by Claire Philpott.— 1st
American ed.
p. cm. — (Bamboo & friends)
Summary: Bamboo and Velvet are sad when Beak says he is not
going to sit on their log with them anymore because birds belong
in trees.
ISBN 1-4048-1301-2 (hardcover)
[1. Rain forests—Fiction. 2. Birds—Fiction. 3. Pandas—Fiction.
4. Zebras—Fiction.] I. Philpott, Claire, ill. II. Title. III. Series.
PZ7.L41835Tre 2005
[E]—dc22   2005008722

2

Bamboo, Velvet, and Beak sit on their log in the middle of the magical forest, just as they always do.

"I have something important to say," says Beak.

4

"Good," says Velvet.
"We're all ears."

Many puffins live near Iceland.

"I'm moving out," announces Beak. "I won't be sitting here on the log anymore. I'm going to sit in a tree."

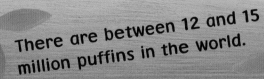

There are between 12 and 15 million puffins in the world.

8

"You're what?" squeal Bamboo and Velvet. "You can't leave the log. This is where we always sit. This is where we belong."

"Birds belong in trees. They don't sit around on logs," says Beak.

"A tree is a kind of town for birds. Birds build their nests there among the leaves. They peck insects from the bark."

Beak continued,
"They curl up and
sleep there, eat there,
and lay their eggs there.

Both the male and female puffins keep the egg warm and care for the chick.

And when the eggs hatch, they raise their chicks there."

"Ah!" says Bamboo.
"That's what all this is about.
You're having a baby."

"I am not!" replies Beak sharply. "It's not about babies. It's about being a proper bird!"

As a puffin becomes an adult, its beak and feet turn a bright shade of orange.

"But birds sit all over the place," argues Velvet. "On buildings, on telephone wires ...

on lampposts,
and on
clothes lines."

"And we'll miss you," adds Velvet sadly.

"You'll be back," says Bamboo. "That tree is pretty crowded with squirrels, woodpeckers, insects, creeping vines, and noisy parrots."

"He's right," says Velvet. "There's the perfect amount of space on this log. A space for Bamboo, a space for me, and a space for you."

For Rent

"Oh, OK," says Beak. "Velvet is right. Birds sit everywhere. I would miss sitting here with my friends."

"Of course you would," says Velvet. "It's where we all belong."

It takes about six weeks for a puffin egg to hatch.

For Rent

Fun Facts

- Puffins swim by using their wings as flippers and their feet as rudders.

- Most adult puffins can fly 48 to 55 miles (77 to 88 kilometers) per hour. The puffin beats its wings approximately 400 times a minute to reach this speed.

- Puffins often live 20 years or more. The oldest known puffin lived to be 29 years old.

- Male puffins are usually slightly larger than females.

- The puffin weighs about as much as a can of soda.

- Adult puffins eat mostly small fish.

- A puffin can dive for up to a minute, but most dives usually last 20 to 30 seconds.

- Giant pandas are usually quiet. When they do make a sound, they bleat rather than growl like other bears.

- Giant pandas are good climbers.

- Giant pandas often take afternoon naps high in the trees.

- Zebras take dust or mud baths to get clean instead of a bath with water!

- The zebras' habitat is the grassy plains, or savannas, of Africa.

On the Web

FactHound offers a safe, fun way to find Internet sites related to this book. All of the sites on FactHound have been researched by our staff.

Here's how:

1. Visit www.facthound.com

2. Type in this special code for age-appropriate sites: 1404813012

3. Click on the FETCH IT button.

Your trusty FactHound will fetch the best sites for you!

Look for all of the books about Bamboo & Friends:

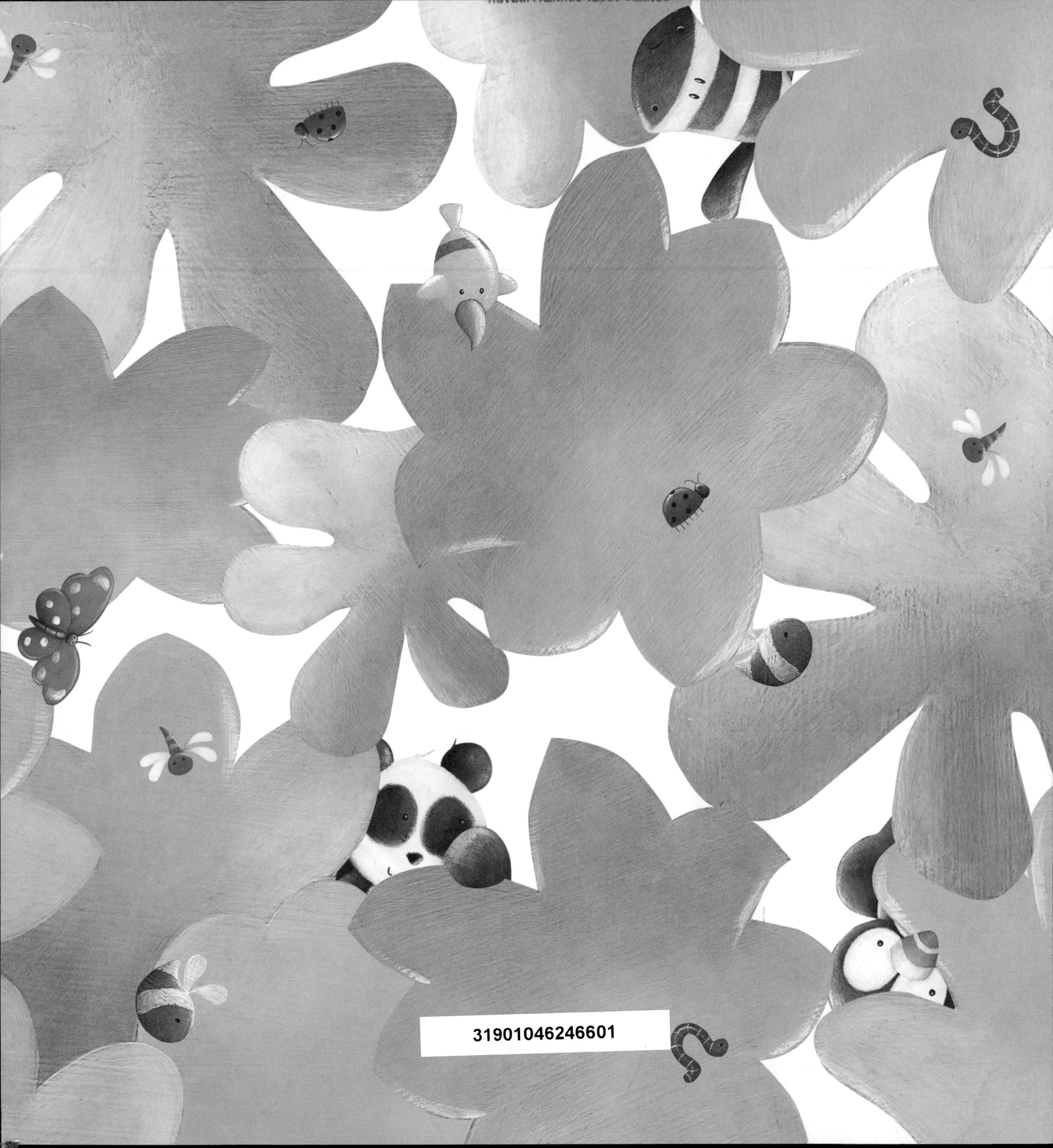